ZIGAZAK!

A Magical Hanukkah Night

ERIC A. KIMMEL

ILLUSTRATED BY JON GOODELL

A DOUBLEDAY BOOK FOR YOUNG READERS

A Doubleday Book for Young Readers
Published by Random House Children's Books
a division of Random House, Inc.
1540 Broadway, New York, New York 10036
Doubleday and the anchor with dolphin colophon are trademarks of Random House, Inc.
Text copyright © 2001 by Eric A. Kimmel
Illustrations copyright © 2001 by Jon Goodell

Cataloging-in-Publication Data is available from the Library of Congress.
ISBN 0-385-32652-1 (trade)   0-385-90004-X (lib. bdg.)

The text of this book is set in 14-point Cochin. · Book design by Trish P. Watts
Manufactured in the United States of America · September 2001
10 9 8 7 6 5 4 3 2 1

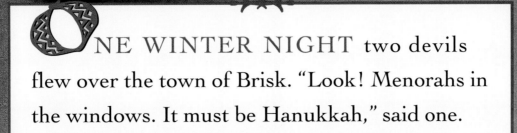

ONE WINTER NIGHT two devils flew over the town of Brisk. "Look! Menorahs in the windows. It must be Hanukkah," said one.

"Let's have some fun," the second devil said.

Together they flew down to Brisk.

They peeked in the window of a large house. It belonged to Zev Wolf, the butcher.

His children were sitting around the table, trying to get all five of their dreidels to spin at once.

"Zigazak!" said the first devil. The dreidels sprouted arms and legs. They formed a circle and began to dance.

"Mama!" the children screamed. Zev Wolf's wife came running. She let out a yell when she saw the dancing dreidels. She gathered her children and ran from the house.

"That was good! Now it's my turn," the second devil said.

They flew to Hannah Leah's house. The old woman stood in the kitchen, frying latkes on the stove.

"Zigazak!" said the second devil. Hannah Leah's latkes rose from the pan and began flying around the room. "Help!" Hannah Leah yelled. She ran out the door without taking off her apron.

"This is fun," the devils laughed. "Let's do some more."

They flew to the house of Menachem Mendel, the richest man in town. The devils peeked in the window. The parlor was filled with guests. A band played. A beautiful menorah with blue-and-white candles stood on the mantel.

The musicians put down their instruments. "And now, honored guests, it is time to light the menorah," Menachem Mendel announced.

He lit a candle and said the blessings.

"Zigazak!" both devils said together. KABOOM! The candles exploded like fireworks. Rockets of colored flame shot to the ceiling, bursting into stars and clusters. The musicians' instruments flew from their hands. Trumpet, clarinet, fiddle, and drum floated in midair, playing a lively *kazatzka*, while sparkling lights swirled around them.

Menachem Mendel was the first one out the door. His family rushed after him, followed by the guests, the cook, the servants, the cat, and all the musicians. Their instruments, still floating around the parlor, played one Hanukkah song after another.

The devils flew all over Brisk, working their mischief in house after house. "Help!" people cried. "Brisk is bewitched!"

"Only the rabbi can save us!" shouted Hayyim Mottel, the school-teacher. The devils had cast a spell over his cat. She had sprouted wings and was now flapping around the house, swooping after the dog.

"The rabbi!" cried Hannah Leah. "Evil spirits have no power over him!"

Everyone ran to the rabbi's house. Dancing dreidels, flying latkes, and exploding candles chased them through the streets.

The rabbi of Brisk was a wise and holy man. As he prepared to light the Hanukkah candles, he suddenly heard a commotion in the street. He opened the door. The people of Brisk swarmed into his house.

"Dear friends, what is wrong? You look terrified," the rabbi said.

Menachem Mendel spoke first. "Help us, Rabbi! Evil spirits are loose in Brisk. Dreidels dance. Latkes fly. Musical instruments play all by themselves. Candles go off like fireworks. Everything is topsy-turvy."

The rabbi looked out the window. "I don't see anything. Surely you are imagining these things."

"No, Rabbi. We saw them with our own eyes. You will see them too. Look!" Zev Wolf took a dreidel from his pocket. He spun it on the rabbi's table. The dreidel sprouted arms and legs. It began to dance.

Everyone screamed. Except the rabbi. He laughed and clapped his hands. "Delightful!" he exclaimed. "Show me more."

Bayla Esther, the rabbi's wife, came in from the kitchen carrying a tray filled with latkes and bowls of applesauce and sour cream. She let out a yell when she saw the dreidel. The tray flew from her hands. But nothing fell. The tray and everything on it floated around the room. The people of Brisk cringed. They pressed themselves against the walls to get out of the way. But not the rabbi. He caught a latke as it flew by, dipped it in a floating bowl of applesauce, and ate it.

"Delicious!" he said.

"Rabbi! Aren't you going to do anything?" Hannah Leah pleaded.

"Of course," said the rabbi. "I'm going to light the Hanukkah candles. It's time." He said the blessings and lit the menorah.

KABOOM! Pinwheels of fire shot from the candles, showering sparks in all directions. Everyone in the room dived under the table. Except the rabbi. He watched the display with astonished eyes, clapping his hands with delight.

"How beautiful! More! More!"

"Rabbi, don't you understand?" Hayyim Mottel pleaded. "Evil spirits are loose in Brisk. You must do something about them."

"Perhaps you're right. I will find out who is behind this." In a deep voice the rabbi commanded, "Evil spirits, if you are present, show yourselves."

The two devils suddenly appeared before the rabbi of Brisk. Everyone in the room covered their eyes. But not the rabbi.

"Creatures of darkness, do you know why I summoned you?"

"You're going to send us off to some desolate wilderness. Do what you like. You can't keep us there. We'll be back."

"You mistake my intentions," said the rabbi. "I summoned you here to thank you for this wonderful magic. It has made our Hanukkah truly special. However, you forgot about Hanukkah gelt."

"What's that?" the devils asked.

"Hanukkah gelt is money. On all eight nights of Hanukkah our children receive coins as gifts. We also give charity to the poor. It would be nice to have some Hanukkah gelt for the children and the poor people in town." The rabbi sighed. "But I suppose that's beyond your powers."

"That's what you think!" said the devils. "Zigazak!"

A waterfall of money rained down from a crack in the ceiling. Gold and silver coins rolled all over the floor. The children ran to catch them.

"Don't touch those coins! They're bewitched!" Hannah Leah screamed.

"Nonsense!" said the rabbi of Brisk. "This money is good. It will remain good long after Hanukkah is over."

"What makes you so sure?" the devils said.

"Nothing is completely wicked," the rabbi replied. "Sparks of holiness exist in all things. Even in devils and their mischief. You came here to spoil our Hanukkah, but by recognizing what was beautiful and delightful in your tricks, I made them good. Your magic has given us the most exciting Hanukkah ever. For this I thank you. Will you accept a Hanukkah gift from me in return?"

"What is it?" the devils asked.

"I can break your chains," said the rabbi. "I can free you from the forces of darkness and turn you into spirits of light. Will you let me?"

"No!" shrieked the devils. "We don't want to be good. We like being wicked. We enjoy spreading trouble wherever we go."

"In that case, you must leave," said the rabbi. "This is a holy night. Evil spirits have no part in it."

"We'll go," the devils said. "But we're taking everything with us . . . menorahs, candles, latkes, dreidels, gelt. Whatever our magic touched belongs to us."

"Oh, no," said the rabbi. "Nothing belongs to you. When magic creates good, it stays good. The forces of darkness no longer possess it."

"Give back what is ours!" the devils screamed. "If you refuse, you'll be sorry. We'll tear this town apart until nothing remains."

The people of Brisk moaned with fear. "Give them what they want, Rabbi, or they'll destroy us!"

But the rabbi of Brisk remained firm. "Do your worst," he told the devils.

"Zigazak!" the devils shouted together. At once they became two ferocious lions.

The rabbi lit his pipe. "I'm not afraid of lions," he said.

"Zigazak!" The devils turned into two hideous monsters.

The rabbi puffed smoke in their faces. "I'm not afraid of monsters either."

"What *are* you afraid of?" the devils asked.

The rabbi shuddered. "I hate to even say the word." He leaned forward and whispered. "Cockroaches. I'm terrified of cockroaches."

"Cockroaches?" The devils looked at each other and winked. "Zigazak!"

At once they turned into two giant cockroaches. Antennae waving, they scurried toward the rabbi.

CRUNCH!

The rabbi lifted his foot. Everyone expected to see two squashed bugs. They saw nothing.

"Where are the cockroaches?" the children asked.

"There were no cockroaches," the rabbi explained. "Those devils took the form of cockroaches to work mischief. When I crushed their forms, they lost their power. They won't be back. Now let's have Hanukkah!"

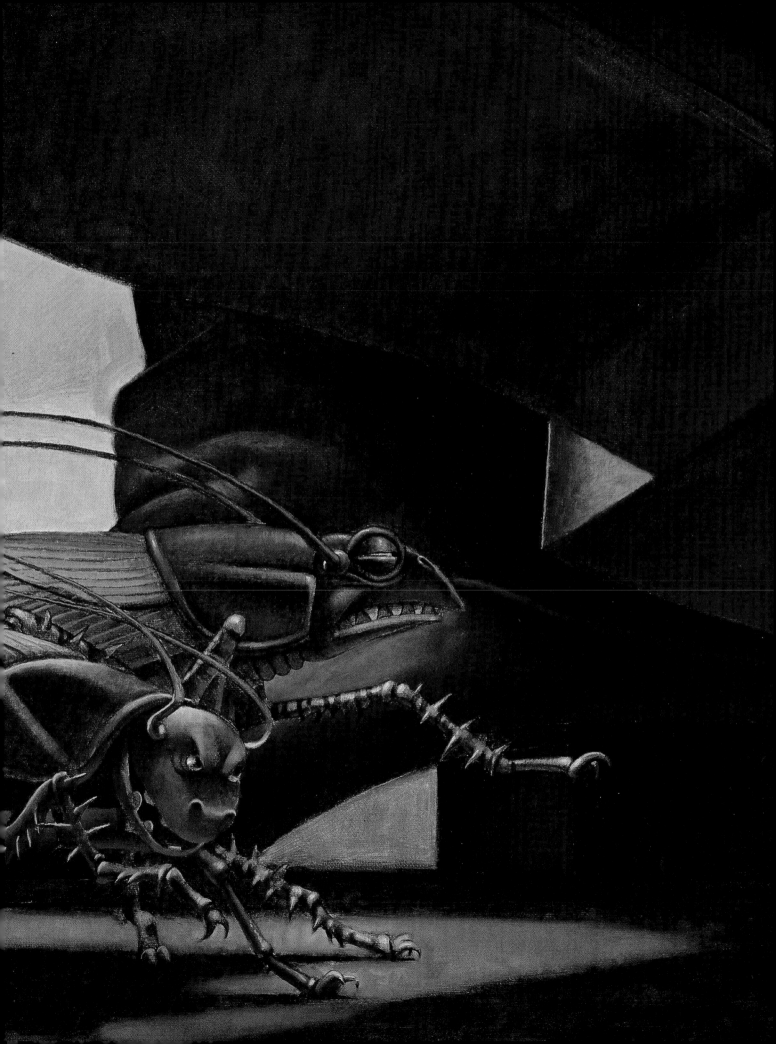

THAT NIGHT the people of Brisk celebrated Hanukkah as never before—with dancing dreidels, flying latkes, skyrocketing candles, cascades of Hanukkah gelt, and musical instruments that played all by themselves. Everyone lit their menorahs outdoors, filling the sky with bursts of spectacular fireworks.

For as the rabbi of Brisk taught, sparks of holiness exist in all things, even in devils' tricks. And if we look hard enough, we can find the good in all living creatures.

Even cockroaches.